Camilla
the Cupcake Fairy

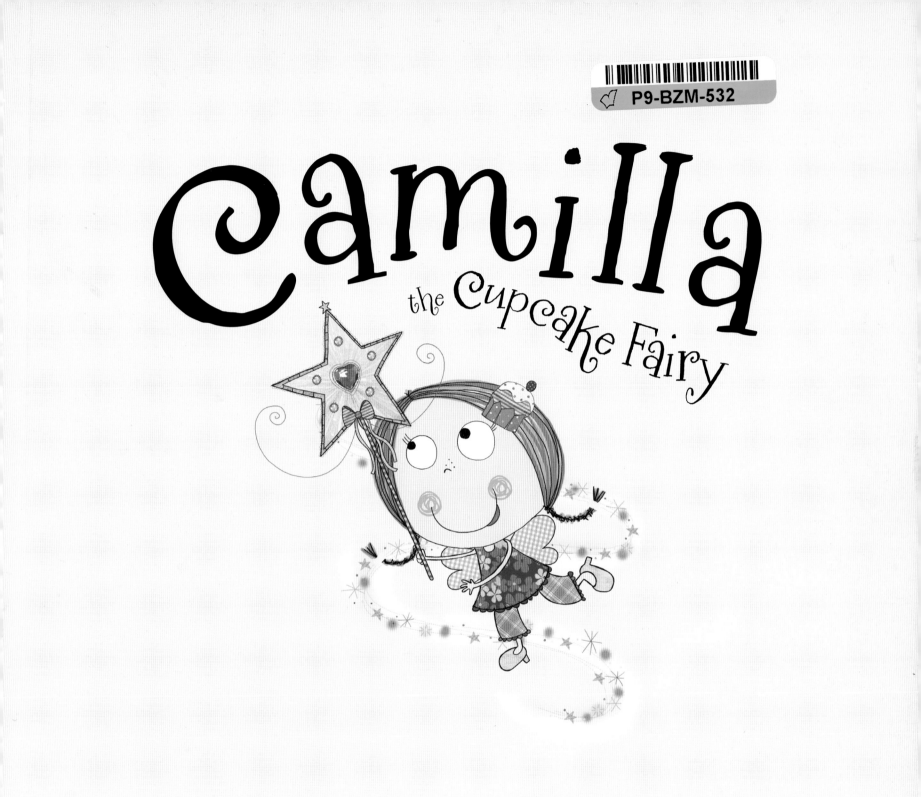

Tim Bugbird · Lara Ede

make
believe
ideas

On **Camilla's** fifth birthday,

the Pink Fairy Post

sent to Camilla what she

dreamed of most.

Not a **hat,** or a **doll,** or a **plant** in a pot,

or anything else she'd already got.

fairy garden

She **tore** off the paper and **giggled** with glee.

"A **wand**!" cried Camilla.

"And meant just for **me**!"

It was so very shiny and sparkly and new.
Her very first wand! But **what** would it **do**?

If she **waved** it carefully
and closed her eyes **tight**,

could she wish for a **party** with **dancing** all night?

Or if she sat nicely,
not making a noise,
would it make her bed neatly
and put away toys?

Or would it put on a **show** with a _dancing_ dog,

The answer was no!
But what it would make,
Camilla was told, was
frosting for cake!
So she found a plain cupcake,
which she placed by her feet,
her wand at the ready,
to make a pink treat!

And holding the **wand**, Camilla stood straight.

She took a deep breath but just **could not wait** . . .

She waved it so fast,

the wand would not stop

whirling and twirling

and flashing on top!

It jumped and it jerked,

with a rattle and a shake,

it jiggled and it juddered

'til she thought

it would break!

Then, with a BANG,

bright stars filled the air.

She looked for

sweet frosting,

but the cupcake was bare!

And there on the top,

not making a sound,

was a tiny white

mouse,

with eyes bright

and round!

So she started again, this time *taking care* to wave the wand gently. But look what was there!

Covering the cake where

the frosting should be . . .

mashed potato was all she could see!

So she tried one more wave, not too fast or too slow.

Now topping the cake there was nothing but . . . . snow!

Well, snowballs and snowmen
she didn't much mind,
but this fancy frosting
was just the
wrong kind!

"Oh dear," thought Camilla.
"This just isn't right.
My wand is not working,
I'll be here all night!"

But then, when it seemed she was down on her luck,

Ms. Sprinkles drove by in her pink fairy truck.

Camilla asked nicely, "What should I do?"

Her teacher said kindly, "I'll give you a clue!"

"Working alone is never much fun,
but with help from your friends, the job is soon done!"

So she called her **friends** on her pink **fairy** phone.

Molly and **Maya** were glad to be home.

Said Molly to Maya, "Our friend's in a state! Let's **fly** to Camilla, this problem **won't wait!**"

They held the **wand** steady
with eyes closed tight.

As they worked hard together,
it shone a **bright** light.

Then crossing their fingers
in a shower of gold **twinkles,**

they all **wished** together

for frosting and
sprinkles!

All of a sudden,
the fairy friends found
the tastiest **treat**,
just there on the ground.

With sparkling

sprinkles

and frosting

so **sweet**,

the **best-ever**

cupcake

was right at their feet!

So the **wand** could work wonders, but nothing compared to the gift of **true friendship** the three **fairies** shared!